LITTLE PORCUPINE'S WINTER DEN

by Susan Thompson-Hoffman

Illustrated by Jennifer Haberstock

Soundprints

A Division of Trudy Management Corporation
Norwalk, Connecticut

For Valerie, dream-weaver,
who has been so much a part of my work.

— S.T.-H.

To Mom and Dad for all their encouragement
throughout the years.

— J.H.

10 9 8 7 6 5 4 3 2
Printed in Singapore

Library of Congress Cataloging-in-Publication Data

Thompson-Hoffman, Susan.

Little Porcupine's winter den / written by Susan Thompson-Hoffman ;
illustrated by Jennifer Haberstock.
                p.   cm. — (Smithsonian wild heritage collection)
Summary: A young porcupine grows up fast on the north rim of
the Grand Canyon as she seeks shelter from plunging temperatures
and fierce winds and protects herself from the many dangers of her
wilderness habitat.
                ISBN 0-924483-64-4
    1. Porcupines—Juvenile fiction. [1. Porcupines—Fiction.]
I. Haberstock, Jennifer, ill. II. Title. III. Series.
                PZ10.3.T378Li   1992
                [E]—dc20   92-14295
                                                                                                        AC

2

Scritch. Scratch. Scritch. Scratch. Wibble, wobble, scritch, scratch. Little Porcupine moved from one buckbrush shrub to the next, nibbling the last of its fruit.

A cold
blast of wind ruffled
the trees along the rim of the
Grand Canyon. Little Porcupine
shivered, rattling her thousands of quills.
For seven days and seven nights,
Little Porcupine had felt the
frigid chill. It was time
to go to her
den.

Little Porcupine's den was a dark, safe place tucked into the side of a rocky hill overlooking the canyon. She had found it when she first ranged beyond her mother's woods. Now it would protect her from fierce winds and icy temperatures.

As Little Porcupine hurried along, coyotes howled in the distance, calling to one another in the night.

She rounded the bend
of the trail. There, above the
path, she saw her den. It was a limestone
cave that sparkled in the moonlight.

As she started up the small rise toward the opening, a large, male porcupine came out of the den. Little Porcupine quickly lowered her head and shoulders. Her quills bristled. The large male raised his quills too, and he barred the den's entrance. When Little Porcupine took two more steps toward him, he screeched shrilly. Little Porcupine turned and scurried to safety below the rim.

As she reached the path once again, she heard
Coyote in the underbrush and she scrambled
for the nearest tree. Flattening her body and
tightening her tail against the bark, Little Porcupine
climbed quickly. Just as she pulled herself up
to a safe branch, Coyote jumped at the tree and
scrabbled with his front paws trying to reach her.
Little Porcupine raised her head and shrieked into the
early dawn. All that day she slept in the abandoned nest
of a tassel-eared squirrel.

The following evening, while Little Porcupine was eating
pine bark, a great horned owl swooped onto a branch
above her. Startled, she scrambled for cover. The owl
never saw her because he was stalking a bushy-tailed
woodrat on the ground. But, in her hurry to escape,
Little Porcupine slipped and fell to the forest floor below.

Slowly, she
crawled back to the
base of the tree. She
had hurt one of her
hind legs in the
fall, and now she found
that she could not use it to climb.

Dragging her sore leg, Little Porcupine started back toward her den once again. She needed shelter. This time, when she reached the cave on the canyon rim, there was no sign of the large porcupine. Little Porcupine sniffed the air and grunted before she entered the den. Licking the leg that hurt, she rested in the opening. When she began to feel hungry again, she limped out for food.

Just as she began to eat, Coyote appeared in a clearing in front of her. He was thin and hungry. Quills rose around Little Porcupine's body.

Coyote opened his mouth and lunged as she quickly
turned to strike him with her tail.

But Coyote was not lunging for her. He was after the large, male porcupine that Little Porcupine had found in her den. He, too, had been feeding on the ground, but now he scrambled up the closest aspen tree. Coyote's teeth glistened as he snapped at the large porcupine just out of his reach.

Moving slowly and quietly, Little Porcupine retreated and hid in a clump of mountain mahogany bushes.

Heavy snow
began to fall.

Coyote waited under the
tree, never taking his yellow eyes off the large porcupine.

Suddenly, a branch that Little Porcupine was leaning against snapped! Coyote spun around and spotted her. Her quills rose up around her and her teeth began to clatter. From his high roost in the aspen tree, the large porcupine peered into the bushes. He, too, saw Little Porcupine.

Her strong, pungent,
warning smell filled the air.

Coyote leaned back on his hind
legs and sprang. Little Porcupine spun
around and whipped her strong tail from side to side.
Coyote let out a savage yelp as her quills pierced
his paws. Whimpering in pain, he limped off.

Slowly,
Little Porcupine
wobbled back to the cave.
Once safely inside, she licked her sore leg and nestled
herself into a hollow in the rock. Shortly after, the
large porcupine appeared at the entrance of the den.
Little Porcupine did not bar the entrance. The large
porcupine came in quickly and retreated to
the back of the cave where he, too, rested.

A single shaft of moonlight pierced the den's opening. It came to rest on Little Porcupine's thousands of quills. Stiffening her back and tail, her quills rose about her.

As she relaxed, they fell smoothly into place against her body. Then she closed her eyes and drifted off to sleep.

About the Porcupine

Porcupine young are born already equipped with quills pressed flat against their bodies. Almost always single births, the young nurse for several weeks and then begin to browse for buds, leaves, fruit, seeds, or inner bark. Porcupines den in caves, under rocks, or in hollow tree stumps in Canada, Alaska, and the western, northeastern, and north-central areas of the United States.

Glossary

aspen: a kind of poplar tree with leaves that flutter in the lightest wind.

buckbrush: shrub growing up to 3 feet tall, often forming thickets; the branches are spiny; the leaves are downey and whitish below, nearly smooth above; the fruit is a small capsule available in fall.

bushy-tailed woodrat: a small rodent with large ears and a bushy tail, also known as the mountain pack rat because of its habit of collecting shiny objects.

cave: a natural, underground space that can be reached from outside.

coyotes: small canids (dog-like animals), native to North America and well-known for their unique howls.

den: a hollow space lived in by wild animals.

horned owl: an owl with tufts of feathers on its head.

limestone: rock formed primarily of organic remains such as shells or coral.

mountain mahogany bushes: thick, deciduous shrubs.

quills: porcupine's defensive weapon—stiff and hard with a sharp point and barbs that make them difficult to remove.

shelter: protection.

Points of Interest in this Book

buckbrush *(p. 3)*

pinon pine *(cover, pp. 5, 6, 12-15, 20)*

horned owl *(p. 13)*

juniper *(p. 16)*

aspen *(pp. 17, 21, 23, 25)*

mountain mahogany *(p. 22)*